MY MOTHER'S HOUSE, MY FATHER'S HOUSE

MY MOTHER'S HOUSE, MY FATHER'S HOUSE

by C. B. Christiansen
illustrated by Irene Trivas

ATHENEUM   1989   NEW YORK

The author wishes to thank the Pacific Northwest
Writers Conference and the Society of Children's
Book Writers for their encouragement.

Atheneum
Macmillan Publishing Company
866 Third Avenue, New York, NY 10022
Collier Macmillan Canada, Inc.
First Edition
Printed in Hong Kong

10 9 8 7 6 5 4 3 2 1

Library of Congress Cataloging-in-Publication Data
Christiansen, C.B.
My mother's house, my father's house.
Summary: A child describes having two different
houses in which to live, "my mother's house" and
"my father's house," and what it is like to travel
back and forth between them.
[1. Divorce — Fiction.   2. Parent and child — Fiction]
I. Trivas, Irene, ill.   II. Title.
PZ7.C45285My 1989 [E]   88-16802
ISBN 0-689-31394-2

To my suitcase friends,
especially Benjamin.
And to Roger.
—C. B. C.

To Lee Chapman
—I. T.

My mother's house has seven rooms and one of
them is mine. I have a closet for my bat and ball
and skateboard and skis. I ride my bike to school.
My mother believes in exercise.

My father's house has three big rooms and parts of each are mine. I have my own desk, a drawer in the dresser, and a bed by the fireplace. In the morning, my bed folds into a couch. My father likes things neat.

When I grow up, I'll have a house with five rooms, a fold-out couch, and a closet for my bat and ball and skateboard and skis. I'll ride my bike to work and pick up after myself.

My mother's house is filled with pictures. Her camera clicks while we climb trees and visit the zoo and plant our pumpkin seeds. My mother's refrigerator is covered with snapshots and a finger painting I made when I was four. Beside her bed, in a silver frame, is a photograph of my mother and me, together.

My father's house is filled with books. His reading glasses bounce on his chest when we walk to the park for a picnic. They rest on his nose when we visit the library. Before he goes to sleep, he puts them on his nightstand by the ashtray I made when I was five. Beside the ashtray is a leather scrapbook with photographs of my father and me, together.

When I grow up, I'll have a house with books
on the tables and pictures on the refrigerator. I'll
visit the library and take picnics to the zoo. On
my bedroom wall I'll hang a photograph of my
mother and my father and me, together.

Before I go to my mother's house on Monday, Tuesday, Wednesday, and Thursday, my father tells me, "Don't forget to brush your teeth and say your prayers and mind your mother."

I pack my suitcase. He adds a roll of dental floss
and my stuffed bear.

Before I go to my father's house on Friday,
Saturday, and Sunday, my mother tells me,
"Don't forget to do your homework and get some
fresh air and mind your father."

I pack my suitcase. She adds a pencil sharpener and my tennis shoes.

When I grow up, I'll live in my house on

Monday . . .

Tuesday . . .

Wednesday . . .

Thursday . . .

Friday . . .

Saturday . . .

and Sunday. I'll have plenty of sharp
pencils and dental floss. But no suitcases.

My mother doesn't go into my father's house. She drops me off at the curb and I run up the steps. She waves from the car window. My father waves back. Our calico cat rubs against my leg and purrs hello. "Welcome home," my father says, as my mother drives away.

My father doesn't go into my mother's house.
He rides the bus with me to the corner where she
lives. I walk half a block to her driveway. Our
two black dogs lick my hand and bark hello.
"Welcome home," my mother says, as my father's
bus rumbles off.

When I grow up, I'll have a house that is
mine, all mine. I'll invite my father to share
my dresser and sleep on my fold-out couch.
I'll invite my mother to dig in my garden
and stay in my extra bedroom.

When I grow up, I'll have two black dogs and a calico cat and a mat on my doorstep that says *Welcome Home*.